Diego Saves the Tree Frogs

adapted by Sarah Willson
based on the original teleplay by Madellaine Paxson
illustrated by Susan Hall

Ready-to-Read

SIMON SPOTLIGHT/NICK JR.
New York   London   Toronto   Sydney

Based on the TV series *Go, Diego, Go!*™ as seen on Nick Jr.®

SIMON SPOTLIGHT

An imprint of Simon & Schuster Children's Publishing Division
1230 Avenue of the Americas, New York, New York 10020
© 2006 Viacom International Inc. All rights reserved. NICK JR., *Go, Diego, Go!*, and all related
titles, logos, and characters are trademarks of Viacom International Inc.
All rights reserved, including the right of reproduction in whole or in part in any form.
SIMON SPOTLIGHT, READY-TO-READ, and colophon are registered
trademarks of Simon & Schuster, Inc.
Manufactured in the United States of America
First Edition
2 4 6 8 10 9 7 5 3 1
Cataloging-in-Publication Data is available for this title from the Library of Congress.
ISBN-13: 978-1-4169-1574-4
ISBN-10: 1-4169-1574-5

Hi! I am .
DIEGO

This is .
BABY JAGUAR

I hear some .
TREE FROGS

They need our help!

Hi,  !

ALICIA

 is my sister.

ALICIA

Hurry,  !

ALICIA

Tell us about  .

TREE FROGS

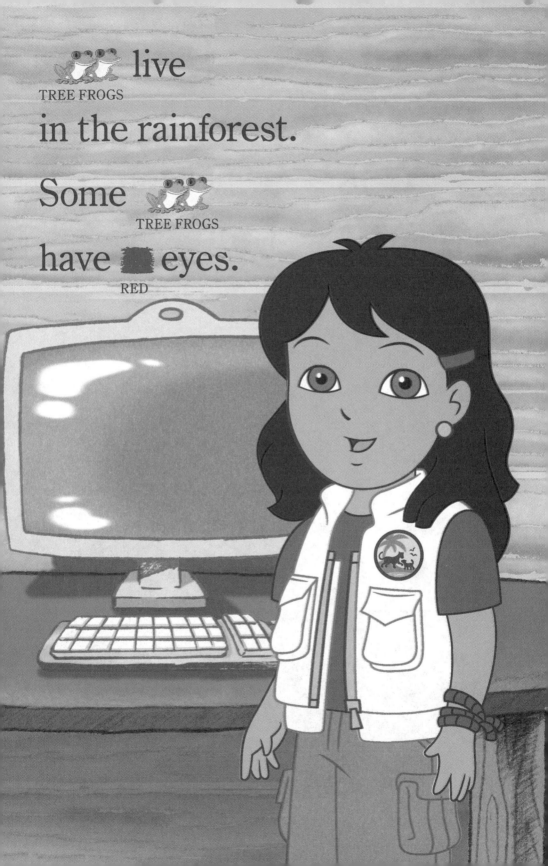

TREE FROGS live in the rainforest. Some **TREE FROGS** have **RED** eyes.

TREE FROGS have strong **LEGS**.

Their **LEGS** help them

to jump high.

 have sticky .

TREE FROGS   TOES

Their  help them

TOES

to climb.

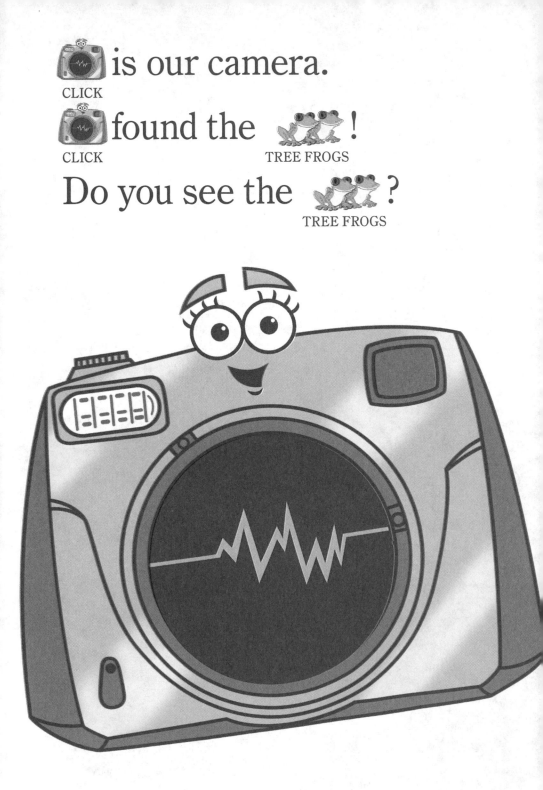

is our camera.

CLICK

found the TREE FROGS!

CLICK

Do you see the TREE FROGS?

The  fell!
TREE FROGS

They are on a ✎.
BRANCH

The ✎ is in the 〰!
BRANCH   RIVER

Come on. We need to save

the  !

TREE FROGS

Look out for the  !
COCONUTS

Jump like a .
TREE FROG

Jump over the !
COCONUTS

The  TREE FROGS went into the PYRAMID.

How will we get inside?

Do you see a DOOR?

I need my sticky .
GLOVES

My  help me climb
GLOVES

like a .
TREE FROG

We made it!

Do you see the ?

Oh, no! The  !
WATERFALL

Tell the TREE FROGS

to jump!

The  jumped.

TREE FROGS

They are safe.

I will take them home.

ALICIA found a new TREE for the TREE FROGS.

The new TREE is strong.
The new TREE is safe.

The  are happy.
TREE FROGS

They love their new .
TREE

We saved the  !
TREE FROGS